Ladybird  Readers

The Tiger, the Brahmin and the Jackal

Series Editor: Sorrel Pitts
Text adapted by Prakash Parmar
Illustrated by Yogita Chawdhary
Song lyrics by Naomi Rainbow

LADYBIRD BOOKS

UK | USA | Canada | Ireland | Australia
India | New Zealand | South Africa

Ladybird Books is part of the Penguin Random House group of companies
whose addresses can be found at global.penguinrandomhouse.com.
www.penguin.co.uk   www.puffin.co.uk   www.ladybird.co.uk

Text adapted from *Tales from India* by Bali Rai, first published by Puffin Books, 2017
This Ladybird Readers version first published by Ladybird Books Ltd, 2022
001

Original copyright © Bali Rai, 2017
Text copyright © Ladybird Books Ltd, 2022
Illustrations copyright © Ladybird Books Ltd, 2022

Printed in Italy

The authorized representative in the EEA is Penguin Random House Ireland,
Morrison Chambers, 32 Nassau Street, Dublin D02 YH68

A CIP catalogue record for this book is available from the British Library

ISBN: 978–0–241–53362–8

All correspondence to:
Ladybird Books
Penguin Random House Children's
One Embassy Gardens, 8 Viaduct Gardens, London SW11 7BW

MIX
Paper from
responsible sources
FSC
www.fsc.org   FSC® C018179

Ladybird Readers

The Tiger, the Brahmin and the Jackal

Adapted from *Tales from India*
by Bali Rai

Picture words

tiger

Brahmin

tree

buffalo

path

jackal

forest

trap

tie

rope

chop down

branch

5

A big tiger lived in a forest in India.

One day, the tiger walked into a trap!

Soon she was tired and hungry.

On the same day, a kind Brahmin came to the forest.

The tiger saw the Brahmin and said, "Brahmin! You must help me!"

"I'm sorry," said the Brahmin. "I can't help you. You want to eat me!"

"No!" said the tiger.
"I'm your friend. Please help me!"

13

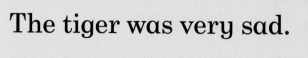

The tiger was very sad.

The Brahmin didn't want her to die.

"OK," said the Brahmin. "I can help you, but please don't eat me."

14

"Thank you," said the tiger.
"Of course not. I don't eat
my friends!"

The Brahmin tied the rope and
opened the trap . . .

"Thanks! Now I can eat you!"
said the tiger.

The Brahmin was very frightened.

"I helped you! Please don't eat me!"
he said.

The tiger thought about it.

Then, she said, "OK, let us find three things and ask them this question: Can the tiger eat me or not?"

First, the Brahmin found a tree.

"Tree! I helped this tiger, but now she wants to eat me! Can she eat me, or not?" he asked.

The tree thought about the question.

"People eat all my fruit and then they chop down my branches. It's not nice!" it said. "Yes, I think the tiger can eat you!"

Then, the Brahmin saw a buffalo in a field.

"Please, buffalo. I helped this tiger, but now she wants to eat me!"
he said. "Can she eat me?"

"When I was young, people were nice to me. I gave them milk and they gave me good food," the buffalo said. "Now I am old. I can't give milk. People give me bad food and I have to work all day in the hot sun! So yes, the tiger can eat you."

The Brahmin was frightened.

"I want to eat you with salt and pepper," the tiger said happily.

The Brahmin looked at the path under his feet.

"Path! I helped this tiger, but now she wants to eat me! Can she eat me?" he asked.

"I am old and thirsty, but people don't give me water," the path said. "They walk on me every day, and I don't like it! So yes, the tiger can eat you."

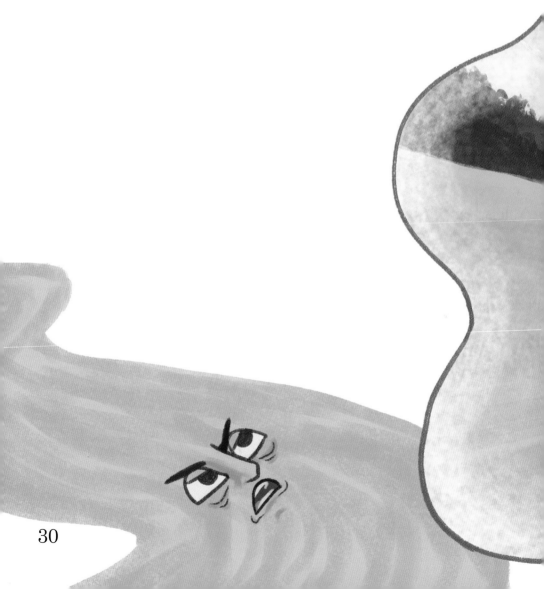

31

The Brahmin was very frightened now.

"OK, eat me, tiger!" he said.

"Come to the forest. I want to eat you there!" said the tiger.

They walked into the forest and met a jackal.

"Hello, Brahmin. Why are you sad?" asked the jackal.

"Leave, jackal!" said the tiger. "This man is my dinner!"

"Why are you the tiger's dinner, Brahmin?" the jackal asked.

The Brahmin told the jackal about his problem.

"I don't understand!" said the jackal. "Was there a trap?"

"Yes!" said the tiger.

"Where is it? Can I see it?" asked the jackal.

The tiger showed the trap to the jackal.

"OK," the jackal said. "The Brahmin was inside . . ."

"No!" said the tiger. "*I* was inside!"

"Oh!" the jackal said. "*I* was inside? I'm sorry, I don't understand. Can you show me?"

"ARRRGGGHHHHHH!"
The tiger was very, very hungry and angry now.

"*I* was *inside* the trap!" said the tiger. "Like this," and she walked into the trap.

"Oh, now I understand!" said the jackal.

Then, the jackal quickly closed the trap.

"Good!" said the jackal.
"Now, Brahmin, go home and
don't talk to any more tigers!"

The Brahmin ran straight home
and the jackal left the forest.

1 **Look and read. Choose the correct words and write them on the lines.** 📖 ✏️ ⭐

tree   trap   buffalo   jackal

1 This has a lot of branches.   tree

2 This animal is very strong.

3 People catch animals in this.

4 This animal has big ears.

2 Circle the correct sentences.

1

a A big tiger lived in a tree in India.

b A big tiger lived in a forest in India.

2

a One day, the tiger walked into a rope!

b One day, the tiger walked into a trap!

3

a Soon she was tired and hungry.

b Soon she was frightened and angry.

4

a A kind Brahmin walked out of the forest.

b A kind Brahmin came to the forest.

3 Talk about the two pictures with a friend. How are they different?

a

b

In picture a, the tiger is in the trap. In picture b, the tiger is out of the trap.

4 Read the story.
Choose the right words and write them on the lines. 📖 ✏️ ✿

1	can't	don't	can
2	my	her	your
3	don't	didn't	not
4	untie	tied	unties

"I'm sorry," said the Brahmin.

"I ¹ ___can't___ help you. You want

to eat me!" "No!" said the tiger.

"I'm ² _____ friend. Please help

me!" The Brahmin ³ _____ want

the tiger to die. He ⁴ _____

the rope and opened the trap.

5 Find the words.

t	i	g	e	r	z	r	e	i
i	c	h	o	p	d	o	w	n
b	r	f	j	q	c	p	k	o
v	c	o	r	b	s	e	y	d
f	b	r	a	n	c	h	j	r
w	r	e	r	y	n	m	d	o
k	l	s	j	z	x	p	t	u
p	a	t	h	h	l	v	g	p

tiger

forest

branch

chop down

rope

path

51

6 Choose the correct words and write them on the lines. 📖 ✏️ ✿

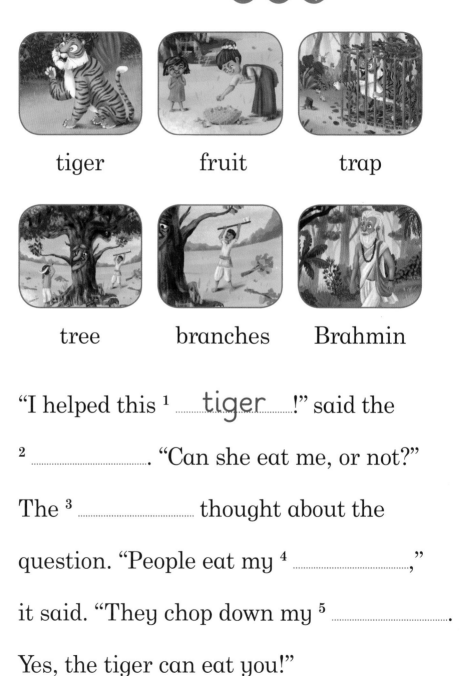

tiger   fruit   trap

tree   branches   Brahmin

"I helped this [1] _tiger_ !" said the

[2] _____. "Can she eat me, or not?"

The [3] _____ thought about the

question. "People eat my [4] _____,"

it said. "They chop down my [5] _____.

Yes, the tiger can eat you!"

7 **Complete the sentences.**
Write a—d. 📖

1 "I helped this tiger,   c

2 "When I was young,

3 "I gave them milk,

4 "I have to work

> **a** people were nice to me."
>
> **b** all day in the hot sun."
>
> **c** but now she wants to eat me!"
>
> **d** and they gave me good food."

8 Circle the correct words.

1 The Brahmin looked at the path
behind / **under** his feet.

2 "I helped this tiger, but now she
wants to **eat** / **catch** me!"

3 "I am old and **thirsty,** / **hungry,**
but people don't give me water,"
said the path.

4 "They walk on me every day,
and I **like** / **don't like** it!"

9 **Read the answers.**
Write the questions.

1 <u>How is the Brahmin feeling?</u>
He is very sad.

2 ....
Yes, she is. She's very hungry!

3 ....

....
They are walking into the forest.

10 Listen, and ☑ the boxes. 🎧 ⭐

1 Who is sad?

 a
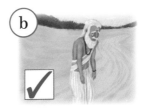 b ✓
 c

2 Who is talking to the Brahmin?

 a
 b
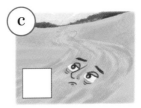 c

3 Where is the tiger?

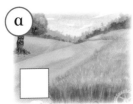 a
 b
 c

4 What can the Brahmin see?

 a
 b
 c

11 Who said this?

Brahmin   jackal   tiger

1 "I can help you, but please don't eat me,"

   said the .... Brahmin ....

2 "I don't eat my friends,"

   said the ....

3 "Can she eat me, or not?"

   asked the ....

4 "I'm sorry, I don't understand. Can you show me?"

   asked the ....

12 **Write the correct questions.**

1 (eat) (Can) (she) (me) (?)

<u>Can she eat me?</u>

2 (sad) (you) (are) (Why) (?)

....

3 (the) (you) (dinner) (Why)

(tiger's) (are) (?)

....

....

4 (I) (Can) (it) (see) (?)

....

5 (me) (show) (you) (Can) (?)

....

58

13 **Look at the picture and read the questions. Write the answers.**

1 Who is angry?

The tiger is angry.

2 Where is the tiger walking?

She is walking _____.

3 Who is the tiger talking to?

She is _____.

14 **Order the story. Write 1—4.**

.... The tiger showed the trap to the jackal.

.... The jackal quickly closed the trap.

.....1..... The tiger and the Brahmin met a jackal.

.... The tiger walked into the trap.

15 **Ask and answer the questions with a friend.** 🗨

1

Where is the tiger?

The tiger is in the trap.

2 What did the jackal say to the Brahmin?

The jackal said "Don't . . .

3 Where did the Brahmin go?

The Brahmin went . . .

16 **Listen, and write the answers.**

1 Did the boy like the story?

.... Yes, he did ....

2 Which animal did the boy like?

....

3 Why did he like this animal?

....

4 Which two things does the boy say?

....

5 Which is the boy's favorite picture?

....

17 Sing the song.

A Brahmin helped a tiger,
She said, "I'm your friend."
Then, she wanted to eat him!
How did the story end?

"Can she eat me, or not?"
The Brahmin asked a buffalo, path and tree.
"Yes, yes, yes!" they all said.
The Brahmin said, "OK, eat me!"

The jackal asked to see the trap,
"Hmm . . . *I* was inside? Can you show me?"
"NO, *I* was inside!" the angry tiger said.
She walked into the trap—"Like this, you see!"

The jackal quickly closed the trap,
The tiger was not their friend.
The jackal helped the Brahmin.
That's how the story ends!